For Stephen, Josie and Raphael and Jay, Max and Jane too – K.Q.

For Elda – P.G.

First published in Great Britain in 2008 and in the USA in 2008 by
Frances Lincoln Children's Books, 4 Torriano Mews,
Torriano Avenue, London NW5 2RZ
www.franceslincoln.com

British Library Cataloguing in Publication Data available on request

ISBN: 978-1-84507-511-8

Illustrated with water colours and ink

Set in Missive

Printed in China

1 3 5 7 9 8 6 4 2

jJ Fic

Fussy Freya

written by
Katharine Quarmby

illustrated by
Piet Grobler

F
FRANCES LINCOLN
CHILDREN'S BOOKS

cucumber

—beans(French style)

Spinach

broccoli

Freya had an appetite
as fine as fine could be.
She'd munch up all her greens for lunch
and **gobble** fish for tea.

tuna

Freya's mum had cooked a dish
of dhal and jasmine rice.
Baby Ravi ate two bowls,

he liked a bit of spice.

Ravi banged the table-top,
   but Freya sulked and glared –
"Your dhal and rice are just not nice,"
   she suddenly declared.

Her mum first sighed a *little*
and then she sighed a lot.
   Did Freya mind a *little*?
   Not a little, not a jot.

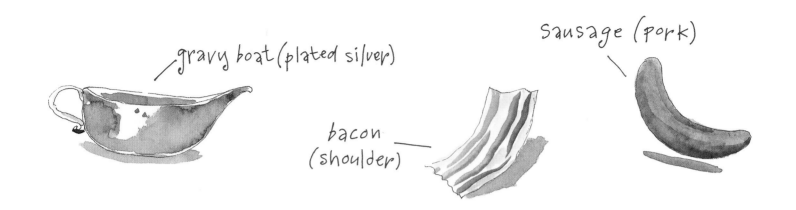

gravy boat (plated silver)

sausage (pork)

bacon (shoulder)

On Tuesday, Freya spurned a plate
of bacon with baked beans,
and **sausages and gravy**
and stir-fried winter greens.

winter greens

Mummy scowled a little
and then she scowled a lot.
Did Freya mind a little?
Not a little, not a jot.

The next day, fussy Freya
let out a frightful roar —
"I can't abide your fish!" she cried
and threw it on the floor.

—heirloom

asparagus

parsley

fish knife

Mummy shrieked a little,
Daddy shrieked a lot.
Did Freya mind a little?
Not a little, not a jot.

parfait
(vanilla)

drumstick
(turkey)

pear
(any)

toffee
apple
(Royal Gala)

By Thursday, fussy Freya
was tucked up in her bed.
Her mummy moaned, her daddy groaned.
"This can't go on," Mum said.

"She's turned down all her favourite food.
She's getting very thin.
I'm worried that she'll soon be
nothing more than bones and skin."

skin

bones

Mum, in despair, phoned Grandma Clare.

"You were the same at three,"

said Grandma Clare to Freya's mum.

"Send Freya here to me."

miaow... ooo...

So Freya packed her weekend bag

to stay with Grandma Clare,

with pink pyjamas, Monkey Monks

and Kanga and Brown Bear.

"What will you eat for tea, my sweet?"
asked Freya's Grandma Clare.

"I'd like giraffe and warthog
and monkey and brown bear."

"You run away and play, my dear.
We'll whip you up a feast."
"We'll sort her," whispered Grandma Clare,
"the fussy little beast."

Freya played with Grandpa's trains
and grinned a wicked grin.
"Perhaps they'll give me lollipops
and sweeties in a tin."

humbugs etc.

train (expensive)

Freya as princess

(profile)   (frontal)

Grandpa came dressed as a chef,
a grin upon his face.
"Please come this way, Princess," he said
and led her to her place.

— sterling silver

Upon the table stood a feast,
a fine and splendid spread
of silver salvers, purple plates —
"Ooh, that looks good!" she said.

— fake snake

zebra hide
(South African)

"You said you'd eat some animals
and then you'd go to bed.
So our first dish is **elephant**
with **egg** upon *its* head."

Grandma laughed a little
and then she laughed a lot.
Did she care when Freya whimpered?
Not a little, not a jot.

"Freya, little darling,
here's **warthog**, if you please.

We serve it here in Norfolk
with a little bit of cheese."

Camembert

Musca domestica

Grandpa laughed a little
    and then he laughed a lot.

Did he care when Freya pouted?
    Not a little, not a jot.

mature cheddar
(very mature)

"Freya, precious poppet, here's mashed monkey with fried rice! We eat it in the summer and we find it very nice."

Freya's lips were quivering –
she wept and shook her head.

"I really want, I'd really like
some butter on brown bread."

Grandpa laughed a little
and Grandma laughed a lot.
"Would you like it served with grilled giraffe
and cream upon the top?"

boiiing

crocodile
(fake)

Freya caught the train next day
With clever Grandma Clare
and Monkey Monks and Kanga,
her pyjamas and Brown Bear.

genuine leather
(lizard)

tea (Earl grey)

pie (any)

Freya ate up all her tea —

"That was good," she said.

"I'm not a fussy eater now."

And then she went to bed.

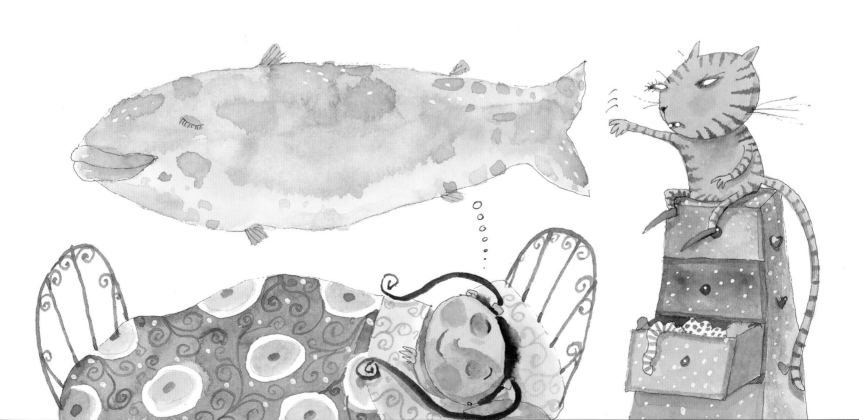

tail (monkey)

wart

And whenever she was fussy,

Dad would ask her in a trice,

"Would you rather eat mashed monkey

on a special bed of rice?

We have it in the freezer

and the warthog's there on ice.

We can heat it in a jiffy

with a sprinkling of spice."

chop
baby potatoes

Daddy laughed a little,
Freya laughed a lot.
Did they cuddle just a little?
No, they cuddled quite a lot!